Produced by Kroha Associates, Inc.
Middletown, Connecticut.

Printed in the United States of America.

ISBN 1-56326-109-X

Minnie's Sleep-Over

By Ruth Lerner Perle

One day, Minnie gave each of her friends a pretty pink invitation.
It read: "Minnie's Sleep-over Party, 5:30 PM Saturday."
"We'll have lots of fun," Minnie said. "And don't forget to bring
your sleeping bags!"

The next day Minnie met Penny on Main Street.

"Hi, Penny!" Minnie said. "What are you doing here?"

"I have to buy a sleeping bag," Penny said. "I've never been to a sleep-over party. What's it like?"

"Oh, we'll have a great time!" Minnie said. "In fact, I'm just going to get some goodies for us to eat at the party."

"Well, uh — I guess I'll see you Saturday night then," Penny said as she waved good-bye.

Minnie was very excited on the day of the party. She had lots of fun things planned for her friends.

Soon the doorbell rang, and all the girls arrived with their suitcases and sleeping bags.

Everybody talked at once as they put their things away, but Penny quietly held on to her stuffed bear.

"I've set up some games we can play!" Minnie said happily. "Come with me!"

Minnie led everyone to the playroom, which was filled with books and games and toys.

First the girls played jacks.

Then they divided into two teams and had a game of charades.

Next they took turns reading scary ghost stories to each other.

And after that they gave all of Minnie's dolls fancy hairdos.

Then everybody gathered around the piano. Daisy played a song they had just learned at school and the girls sang along.

Minnie noticed that everyone seemed to be having a good time. Everyone except Penny.

After awhile, Minnie said, "I guess you must be getting hungry. We're having spaghetti and meatballs for dinner, and chocolate pudding and cookies for dessert."

"Yum!" said Daisy.

"Let's eat!" Clarabelle and Lilly said together.

Penny didn't say anything, but Minnie knew that Penny loved spaghetti and chocolate pudding, too.

All the girls went into the kitchen and helped make the spaghetti, mix the pudding, and arrange the cookies on a plate.

Soon everything was ready and the girls helped carry the food to the table.

"This is a wonderful party," Clarabelle said.

Minnie smiled and said, "It's going to get even better! Since it's such a beautiful night, we can sleep outside in my tent."

"Hurray!" Daisy cried. "I love sleeping outdoors."

"How exciting!" Clarabelle and Lilly chimed in.

Penny just looked worried and hugged her bear even tighter.

The girls sat down at the table and helped themselves to big plates full of spaghetti and meatballs. Everyone was quiet as they hungrily ate their dinner.

"I've never slept away from home before," Penny whispered. She slowly twirled the spaghetti around her fork.

"I felt a little homesick at my first sleep-over, but I had fun, too," Daisy said.

Minnie noticed that when it was time for the chocolate pudding, Penny didn't have any at all.

"I guess I'm not very hungry," Penny said softly.

After dinner, the girls changed into their pajamas and took their sleeping bags out into the tent. They giggled and joked until it got dark, and then they climbed into their sleeping bags.

Penny hugged her bear and looked around. The moon was full and she could hear an owl hooting nearby. She listened to the breeze rustling through the leaves. *Was that a ghost?* Penny wondered.

Penny pulled the sleeping bag up to her chin and shivered. Then she noticed the strange outline the branches made against the wall of the tent. The shadow was shaped like a giant monster.
Penny wished she were home in her own warm bed.

The leaves outside the tent rustled again.
"What was that?" Lilly called out.
"Why? Are you scared?" asked Penny.
"A little," Lilly admitted.
"I am, too!" Daisy said.
"So am I!" said Clarabelle.
Penny was relieved. "I was afraid to say
anything because I thought I was the
only one," she said.
"I guess we all get scared
sometimes," Minnie said.
"And being away from
home can be especially
scary."

Minnie thought for a moment. "I know how we can all feel cozy and safe!" she said.

She ran into the house and came back with a great, big, fluffy quilt.

"Now everybody make a circle with your sleeping bags," Minnie said.

When they were all side-by-side, Minnie covered all five bags with the snuggle-y quilt.

All the girls tucked the quilt in around them and reached out for each other's hands. "Oh, Minnie," Penny said. "I feel so much better now. With you for a friend, a sleep-over party can be fun."

Sometimes it's hard to admit you're afraid — but when friends stick together, even scary things don't seem so bad.

"Good night, everybody," Minnie said.

"Good night, Minnie! Good night, everybody!" Penny whispered softly.

Then Penny sighed a big sigh, and before she knew it, she was fast asleep.

Have you ever felt worried about doing something new or being away from home? Please write and tell me about it and I'll answer your enclosed letter.